First Dinosaur Book

Find out about pterosaurs like me on pages 36–37.
Why did I have bony plates on my back? Find out on page 14.
Learn why dinosaurs like me had huge slashing claws on page 21.
Turn to page 22 to learn how I used my tail for protection.

First Dinosaur Book

Clive Gifford
Consultant: Camilla de la Bédoyère
Illustrated by Ela Smietanka and Ana Gomez

SCHOLASTIC

CONTENTS

I hunted other dinosaurs for my dinner.

I help to dig dinosaur fossils out of the ground.

I've been learning about dinosaur eggs and nests.

What are dinosaurs?

Dinosaurs are ancient land-dwelling reptiles that once roamed the Earth. They died out millions of years ago, but we can learn about them from the traces they left behind.

The word dinosaur means 'terrible lizard'.

What's in a name?

Dinosaurs are often named after how they look, where they were found or who found them. *Herrerasaurus* was named after goat herder Victorino Herrera who first found this dinosaur in Argentina in 1959.

I CAN... SAY THE LONGEST NAME

The longest dinosaur name is... *Micropachycephalosaurus* meaning, 'tiny, thick-headed lizard'! Practise saying the name to impress your friends. It should sound like...

The first dinosaurs

These amazing creatures are thought to be have lived over 230 million years ago. Most early dinosaurs moved around on two legs.

Standing tall

Plateosaurus was a plant-eater that could stand on its back legs to reach leaves way up high.

Small and speedy

Eoraptor was a small but fast two-legged dinosaur. It was about one metre long and weighed 10 kilograms – about the same as a small dog.

Group hunter

Coelophysis could grow to be about as tall as you. This early dinosaur lived and hunted in large groups.

I CAN... MAKE A BALANCING DINOSAUR

Draw, colour in and cut out a dinosaur body from half of a paper plate. Use the other half to make the head, neck and tail. Try clipping on two clothes pegs as legs in different places along the base. Does your dino balance or topple over?

Dinosaur skeletons are really rare. People were amazed when 100 *Coelophysis* skeletons were found all together in the USA in 1947.

When did dinosaurs live?

Dinosaurs lived on Earth between 235 and 66 million years ago in a time known as the Age of Dinosaurs. This is split into three parts, called the Triassic, Jurassic and Cretaceous periods.

Humans weren't alive in dinosaur times, but other animals such as insects, fish, lizards and crocodiles were.

Jurassic

This middle time period was between 200 and 145 million years ago.

Triassic

Dinosaurs first appeared on Earth in Triassic times, between 250 and 200 million years ago.

The first dinosaurs appear. They are small two-legged meat-eaters and larger plant-eaters.

No single type of dinosaur lived throughout the Age of Dinosaurs. Many different kinds came and went.

One big home

When dinosaurs first arrived, all of the land on Earth was clumped together in one big mass called Pangaea. Over time, the land drifted apart, taking dinosaurs to different parts of the planet.

Cretaceous

Lots of dinosaurs lived in Jurassic times, including the gigantic plant-eating sauropods.

Huge meat-eaters and large armoured plant-eaters roamed Earth in the Cretaceous Period.

I CAN... BUILD A DINOSAUR SKELETON

Build a dinosaur skeleton using dried pasta, a piece of card and some glue. Use macaroni tubes and other pasta shapes to form the bones of your skeleton. Why not write your dinosaur's name on the card as well?

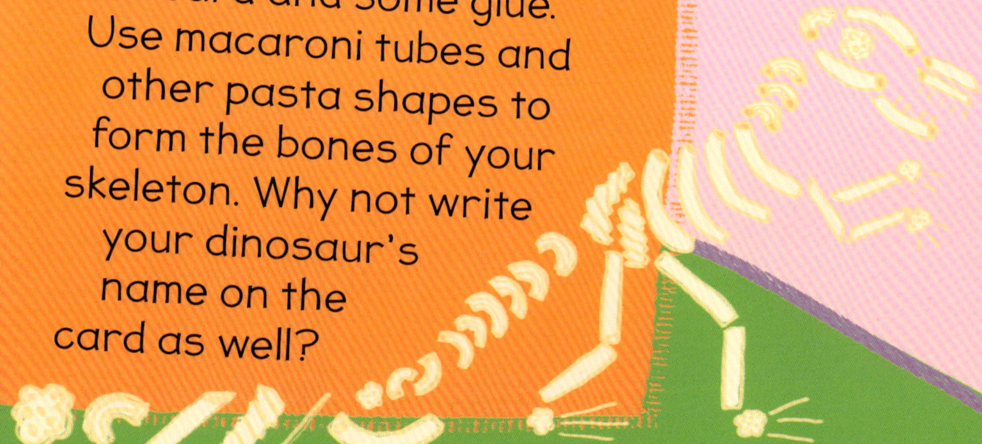

The Cretaceous Period, between 145 and 66 million years ago, was the height of the Age of Dinosaurs.

Shapes and sizes

Dinosaurs came in all kinds of shapes and sizes. Some weighed as much as ten elephants while others were smaller than a chicken.

To pump blood around its huge body, *Brachiosaurus'* heart was probably the size of a dustbin.

I CAN... WORK OUT THE WEIGHT

Weigh yourself and then use a calculator or get an adult to help you work out:

1 How many times your weight equals the daily food of a *Brachiosaurus*?

2 How many of you would weigh as much as a *Giganotosaurus*?

3 How many 4-kilogram *Compsognathus* dinosaurs weigh as much as you?

Great grazers

The prehistoric world was packed with plants, from tall trees to lush bushes and ferns. More than half of all known dinosaur species were plant-eaters, munching on plants all day long to survive.

Slow and strong

Stegosaurus was built like a tank. It weighed up to 3.5 tonnes and moved slowly, eating mostly twigs and leaves.

Spiky thumb

Iguanodon could walk on four legs, but rise up on two to reach taller bushes and trees.

I CAN... MAKE A SWEET STEGOSAURUS

Trim a third off a pancake. Slice some strawberries to make the plates along the back and add half a banana, sliced in two, for a tail. Use pineapple chunks for legs, another strawberry as the head and blueberries for an eye and body decoration. Yum!

Lawnmower mouth

Nigersaurus' mouth contained up to 500 teeth. These cut and chewed up small plants a bit like a lawnmower.

Nigersaurus grew a new set of teeth every few weeks as they wore away quickly.

Meet the meat-eaters

Many dinosaurs hunted other creatures. Some relied on speed and quick reactions to catch creatures. Others used their big size and brute strength.

Spinosaurus

Longer than a school bus, this big beast liked hunting in water. It gobbled up huge fish, spearing them with its long jaws full of sharp teeth.

I CAN... NAME FIVE CARNIVORES

Meat-eating dinosaurs are called carnivores and plant-eaters are called herbivores. Can you think of five carnivores and five herbivores that are around today?

Super-sized sauropods

These dinosaurs were huge plant-eaters. They all had long tails to balance out the long necks that they needed to reach plants way up high.

Heavyweight champion

Argentinosaurus was a 35-metre-long giant and one of the heaviest dinosaurs. It weighed about 70 tonnes, more than five times the size of *T rex*.

***Diplodocus*' long tail was more than half the total length of its body**

Apatosaurus had to eat 400 kilograms of food a day to survive.

Spiny plant-eater

Diplodocus was a 26-metre-long dinosaur weighing about 20 tonnes. It used its peg-shaped teeth to strip leaves off of branches.

I CAN... COMPARE DINOSAUR LENGTHS

Measure the height of one of your friends. Then work out how many of them lying down end-to-end it would take to be as long as *Argentinosaurus*.

Stony stomach

Apatosaurus didn't chew its food but instead swallowed it whole. Like many plant-eaters, it also ate large stones that stayed in its stomach and helped grind the food down.

Teeth and claws

Dinosaur experts love looking at teeth and claws. These things help to tell us lots about how dinosaurs lived and the sorts of things they liked to eat.

Types of teeth

Dino teeth were well-matched to the different sorts of food that dinosaurs ate.

Razor claws

Claws on dinosaurs' hands and feet were used for attack, defence and to gather food.

Therizinosaurus had huge slashing claws on its hands up to one metre in length!

I CAN... CREATE CRAZY DINOSAURS

Draw one half of a dino on the top half of a piece of paper. Make it look as crazy as you like. Fold the paper over so that almost all of your drawing is hidden. Then get a friend to complete the creature. Open the paper to see the finished result.

Horns and armour

Some plant-eating dinosaurs were slow and heavy and couldn't run away from predators. Luckily, they were protected by heavy armour, and some had long horns or clubs too.

Three-horned face

Triceratops was enormous – up to 9 metres long and 3 metres high. A thick, scaly skin and three horns helped protect it from attack.

Bone head

With a big bony dome on its head and a crown of short spikes, *Pachycephalosaurus* butted away predators or rivals.

Triceratops had one of the biggest dinosaur heads – almost a third of its body length.

I CAN... MAKE A TRICERATOPS MASK

Cut one third off a paper plate as shown. Carefully cut out two eyeholes and two small holes at the sides. Next, take some card and cut out three horn shapes and a nose and stick to your plate. Colour your mask and attach some ribbon or elastic to tie it to your head.

Nests and eggs

Dinosaurs hatched from eggs, just like birds and crocodiles today. The smallest dinosaur eggs were just 1.8 centimetres long but others were up to 60 centimetres in length.

Good parents

Troodon parents half buried their eggs in mud in ring-shaped nests. They then sat over the eggs to keep them warm until they hatched.

Covered up

Some dinosaurs covered their eggs with mounds of twigs and leaves. As the mound rotted, it gave off heat, warming the eggs.

Edmontosaurus looked after its nest and protected the babies from predators

I CAN... FIND DINOSAUR NAMES

Hidden within each set of jumbled letters is the name of a dinosaur. Can you unscramble the letters to find them?

sea sours tug
coaster trip
old disco up

Answers: Stegosaurus; Triceratops; Diplodocus

Egg thieves

Eggs and hatchlings were preyed upon by snakes and other dinosaurs.

The snake may have cracked the egg open before it pounced

Dino babies

Most baby dinosaurs had to feed and defend themselves as soon as they hatched. Baby *Maiasaura* were lucky. They had parents who cared for them until they could look after themselves.

Maiasaura grew up fast. By their eighth birthday, they could weigh 2.3 tonnes!

Caring colonies

Plant-eating *Maiasaura* lived together in herds and raised their young in colonies. They brought food to their babies while they were still in the nest.

Protecting their young

Adult *Triceratops* may have protected their young from attack by forming a circle around the youngsters with their heads and horns sticking outwards.

I CAN... GROW UP LIKE A DINOSAUR

Ampelosaurus babies grew from 4 kilos at birth to be a huge 8000 kilos – that's 2000 times bigger! Find out your weight when you were born. Then multiply that figure by 2000. Bet the answer is heavy!

On the move

Just like buffaloes or zebras today, some dinosaurs lived in large herds. This helped to protect individuals from attack by fierce meat-eaters.

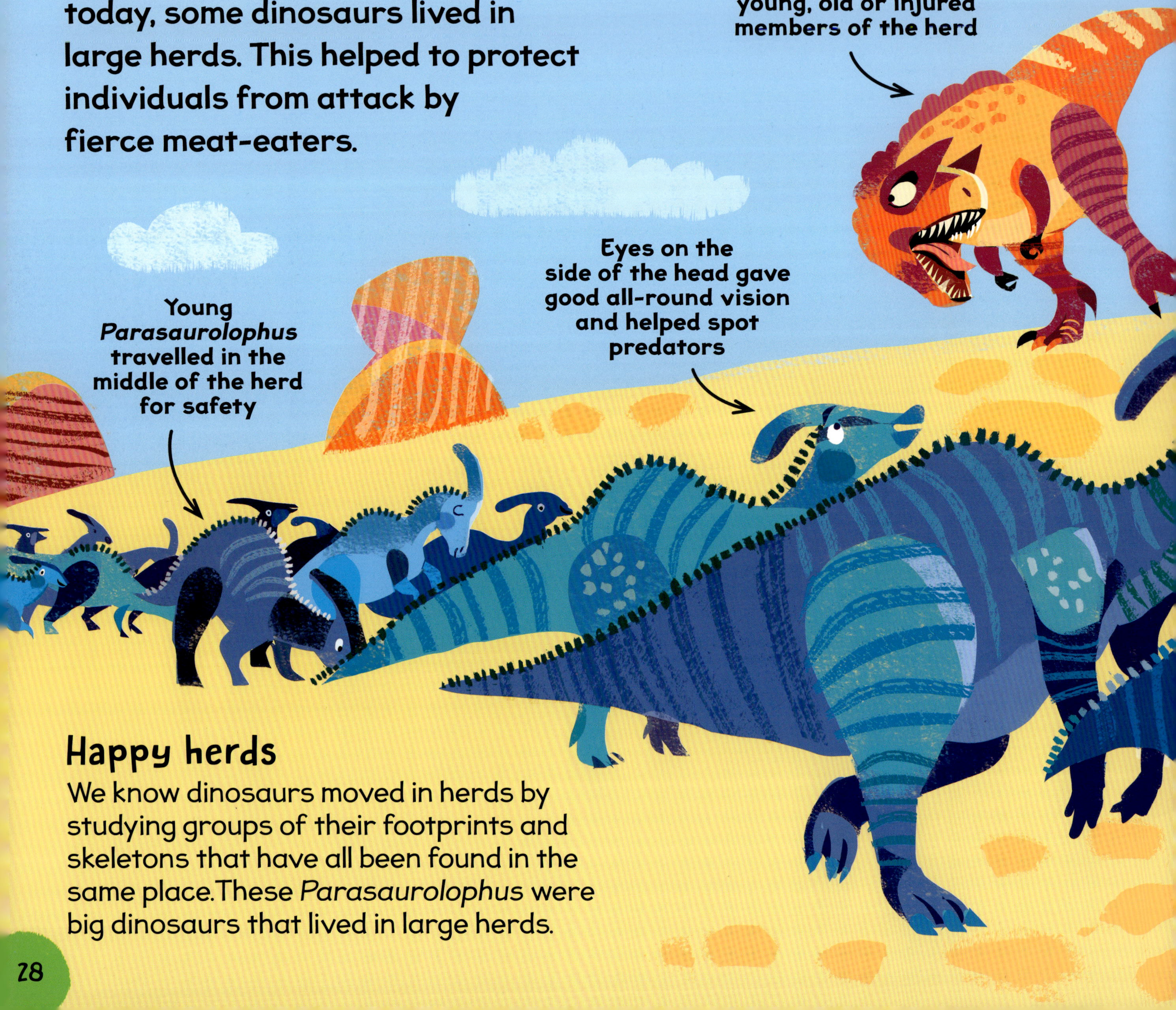

Happy herds

We know dinosaurs moved in herds by studying groups of their footprints and skeletons that have all been found in the same place. These *Parasaurolophus* were big dinosaurs that lived in large herds.

Parasaurolophus' huge crest helped it to make a loud sound like a trumpet, perhaps to warn others.

A vast herd of thousands of *Centrosaurus* skeletons has been found in Canada.

Duck-shaped bill full of teeth ground up tough plants

Young *Parasaurolophus* walked on two legs. As they grew up and got heavier they often walked on all four.

I CAN... MAKE A DINOSAUR ROAR

Take a deep breath and do your best to make a deep, scary roar. Now make a trumpet out of a long cardboard roll and a piece of card shaped into a cone at one end. Make a loud trumpeting sound into it. Which is louder?

Making tracks

All dinosaurs moved on land although some also waded through water. We can learn about how they moved from the fossil footprints they left behind.

Fantastic feet

Dinosaur footprints have been found all around the world. Skeletons found nearby help us to identify which dinosaur the footprints belong to.

***T rex* walked and ran on its toes**

Each of *T rex*'s footprints are about twice the size of an adult man's

The biggest dinosaur footprint, found in Australia, belonged to a huge sauropod. It measured 175 centimetres long and 90 centimetres wide!

Alamosaurus

This heavy dinosaur plodded slowly on its four massive legs

I CAN... MAKE DINOSAUR TRACKWAYS

Design a dinosaur foot and ask an adult to cut a sponge to the same shape. Dip your sponge foot into bowls of poster paint and stamp out a trackway of footprints across a large piece of paper.

Footprints were up to 80 centimetres long

Struthiomimus was a fast dinosaur, reaching speeds of up to 80 kilometres an hour!

Powerful legs

***Struthiomimus* looked a bit like a giant ostrich**

T rex terror!

***Tyrannosaurus rex* is one of the most famous and fierce dinosaurs of all. *T rex* hunted many other dinosaurs but may also have feasted on dead animals that it found.**

T rex teenagers got heavier fast. They could add 2 kilograms to their weight every day.

Jaws of awe

T rex's jaws were 1.2 metres long – about as long as you are tall! When opened wide, its jaws revealed 60 long, sharp, cone-shaped teeth.

A *T rex* skeleton found in 1990, called Sue, was sold for $8.3 million dollars!

I CAN... MAKE MY OWN T REX TEETH

Get a large, curved banana and wrap it in thin, white paper using sticky tape. Now imagine 60 of these curved teeth in a giant mouth. Scary stuff!

Raptor attack

Not all hunters were huge like *T rex*. Raptors were usually small, two-legged meat-eaters with feathers and vicious claws. Many were smaller than you, but they were fierce hunters.

Great glider

Chicken-sized *Microraptor* had arms and legs covered in feathers. It used them as wings to glide between branches.

Fast-moving *Velociraptor* was about the size of a large turkey.

Scary beast

Unusually for raptors, *Utahraptor* was 2 metres tall. It was the biggest raptor of all.

***Utahraptor* weighed over 400 kilograms, making it heavier than a grizzly bear.**

I CAN... SPOT THE RAPTOR

Can you end these six dinosaur names correctly using 'raptor', 'saurus' or 'ceratops'?

Tri_______
Ovi_______
Stego _______
Proto _______
Bambi______
Apato______

Answers: Triceratops; Oviraptor; Stegosaurus; Protoceratops; Bambiraptor; Apatosaurus

Up in the air

Soaring high above dinosaurs on the ground, pterosaurs ruled the air. These prehistoric flying reptiles ranged from the size of a small bird to a small aeroplane.

Pterodactylus flew over seas to feast on small fish.

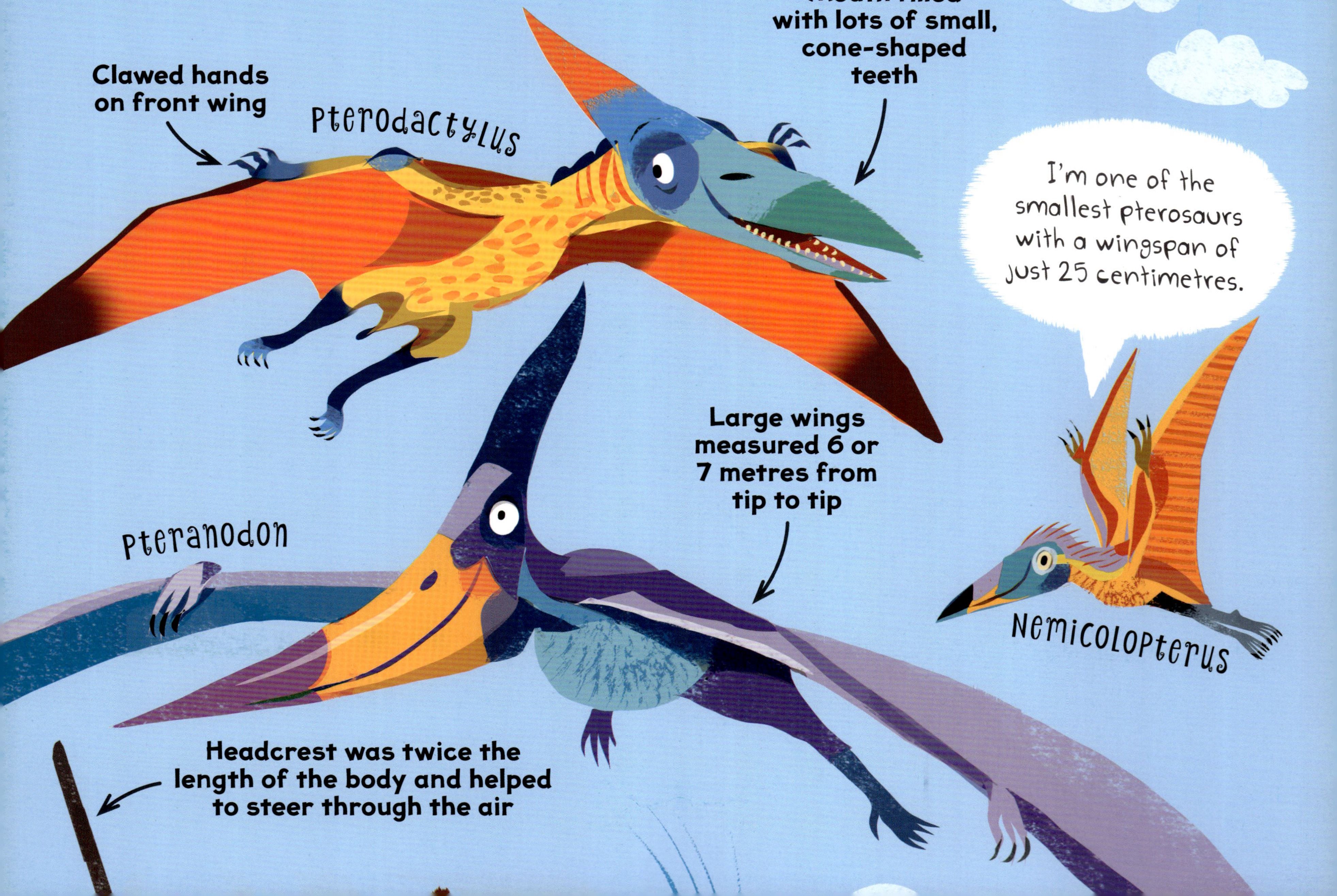

I CAN... DRAW MY OWN PTEROSAUR

Get a big piece of paper and design your own flying reptile. How big would its wings be? What shape would you make its head and tail? What food would it eat? Would it have a crest on its head?

Giant glider

The biggest pterosaur of all was *Quetzalcoatlus*. Its wings could measure 11 metres from tip to tip. That's four times bigger than the bird with the largest wingspan today, the albatross.

Under the sea

While the dinosaurs walked the Earth, huge marine reptiles swam in the seas feasting on fish. These reptiles could dive down deep, but all had to come up for air regularly.

I CAN... MAKE LOTS OF WORDS

Use the word 'OPHTHALMOSAURUS' to create as many new words as you can by rearranging the letters. Each word must be at least two letters long. Use a dictionary to check the spelling of your words.

The end of the dinosaurs

Dinosaurs lived on Earth until about 66 million years ago when they disappeared. This is what we think happened...

① The last dinosaurs

Around 66 million years ago, dinosaurs were still thriving on land. Big beasts like *Triceratops*, *Ankylosaurus* and mighty *T rex* were all still alive.

② Impact!

An asteroid (a large rock from space) struck Earth. It sent huge clouds of dust into the air blocking out the Sun and making Earth much colder and darker than before.

③ Dying out

Earth went through climate change for many years. Lots of plants died out and so did many creatures, including all of the dinosaurs.

④ Survivors

Some creatures survived including crocodiles, turtles, snakes and birds. New animals appeared after the dinosaurs including monkeys, wild cats and us – humans!

Fossil clues

Dinosaurs may have gone but they left behind their remains, which are known as fossils. Most of what we know about these amazing creatures comes from finding fossils.

A fossil leg bone of a sauropod found in France measured a whopping 2.2 metres long!

American George Frandsen has a collection of 1277 fossilized dinosaur poos!

How fossils are made

Fossils take thousands and sometimes millions of years to form. Lying under layers of rock, the dinosaur's skeleton dissolves away. It leaves space which is filled by a stony substance that forms a replica of the dinosaur's bones.

1. A **dinosaur** dies. Its soft parts **rot** away and it gets covered in layers of sand or mud that eventually turn to rock.

2. The dinosaur's **skeleton** dissolves and is replaced with a stony substance, forming a **fossil**.

A **COMPLETE SKELETON** is a very rare and **EXCITING** find.

Trace fossils are things like nests, footprints and dung left behind by dinosaurs.

I CAN... MAKE A FOSSIL

Make a dough by mixing 1 cup of salt with 2 cups of flour and about ½ cup of water. Divide it into six pieces and shape them into flattened rounds, like a cookie. Press shells, toy insects or dinosaurs into the dough, remove and let your fossils dry and harden overnight.

Dinosaur skeletons have to be pieced together, bone by bone, like a jigsaw puzzle.

③ Millions of years later, the rocks have moved or are worn away to reveal the **fossil**.

At the museum

Fancy going face-to-face with real life dinosaur skeletons? What about seeing full-sized dinosaur models move and roar? There's no better place to go than a dinosaur museum.

The Natural History Museum in London, UK, holds sleepovers for kids underneath its giant dinosaur skeletons.

I CAN... MAKE A PREHISTORIC POSTER

Pick a dinosaur, perhaps one from this book, and make your own poster all about it. Draw a large picture of your dinosaur, colour it in and write lots of facts about it in the spaces. Use your school library or ask a teacher to help you learn more.

Fossil hunter

Mary Anning (1799–1847) was just 12 years old when she found an ichthyosaur fossil near her home in southern England over 200 years ago. Mary went on to discover lots of other fossils during her lifetime.

Glossary

Armour
A strong, hard covering that protects a creature from harm.

Asteroid
A chunk of rock in space that travels around the Sun. Some asteroids crash into planets like Earth.

Climate change
When the general weather patterns around the world alter greatly.

Dissolves
When a substance disappears, often through being mixed with water.

Flexible
Something that can bend easily without breaking.

Fossil
The remains of plants and creatures, including dinosaurs, which lived a long time ago. Fossils are often found preserved in rock.

Hatchlings
Very young creatures that have just hatched out of their eggs.

Herd
A large group of animals that live together.

Jaws
The bony parts of any animal's head that hold their teeth.

Predators
Creatures, including dinosaurs like *T rex*, which hunt and kill other creatures for food.

Prehistoric
Times before anything was written down. This period stretches back millions of years.

Prey
Creatures that are hunted and eaten by others.

Pterosaur
A flying reptile from dinosaur times.

Replica
A copy of something that looks very similar to the original.

Reptile
A cold-blooded animal that usually has dry, scaly skin and uses the heat of the Sun to keep its blood warm.

Sauropod
A type of giant plant-eating dinosaur that moved on four legs and had a long neck and tail.

Skeleton
The framework of bones that supports an animal's body.

Tonne
Short for metric tonne, this is a weight equal to 1000 kilograms.

Trackway
A path or trail formed by lots of animals' footprints all following the same route.

Say my name

Dinosaur names can be hard to pronounce. Use this handy guide to learn to say their names.

Dinosaurs

Alamosaurus	A-lam-oh-SORE-us
Allosaurus	AL-oh-SORE-us
Ampelosaurus	am-PEL-oh-SORE-us
Ankylosaurus	an-kee-lo-SORE-us
Apatosaurus	a-PAT-oh-SORE-us
Argentinosaurus	ar-jen-TEEN-oh-SORE-us
Brachiosaurus	BRAK-ee-oh-SORE-us
Coelophysis	see-loh-FIE-sis
Compsognathus	komp-sog-NATH-us
Deinonychus	di-NON-ee-kus
Diplodocus	dip-lo-DOKE-us
Edmontosaurus	ed-MON-toe-SORE-us
Eoraptor	EE-oh-RAP-tor
Gallimimus	gal-lee-MY-mus
Giganotosaurus	jig-ano-toe-SAW-rus
Herrerasaurus	heh-RARE-ra-SORE-us
Iguanodon	ig-WAH-noh-don
Maiasaura	my-a-SORE-a
Microcephalosaurus	MI-kro-sef-alo-SORE-us
Microraptor	MY-crow-RAP-tor
Minmi	min-mee
Nigersaurus	nai-ja-SORE-us
Pachycephalosaurus	pak-ee-sef-alo-SORE-us
Parasaurolophus	para-sore-ROL-oh-fus
Plateosaurus	pla-tee-oh-SORE-us
Spinosaurus	SPY-noh-SORE-us
Stegosaurus	STEG-oh-SORE-us
Struthiomimus	STREW-theo-MY-mus
Tyrannosaurus rex	tie-RAN-oh-sore-us rex
Therizinosaurus	thera-ZINA-SORE-us
Triceratops	tri-SERRA-tops
Troodon	TRUE-oh-don
Utahraptor	U-ta-RAP-tor
Velociraptor	ve-LOSS-ee-RAP-tor

Pterosaurs

Nemicolopterus	NEM-ee-kol-OPT-er-us
Nyctosaurus	NIC-to-SORE-us
Pteranodon	te-RAN-oh-don
Pterodactylus	terra-DACT-aluss
Quetzalcoatlus	ket-zal-KWAT-luss

Marine reptiles

Elasmosaurus	el-lazz-mo-SORE-us
Liopleurodon	LIE-oh-PLUR-a-don
Mosasaurus	moe-za-SORE-us
Ophthalmosaurus	op-THAL-mo-SORE-us
Shastasaurus	SHAZ-ta-SORE-us